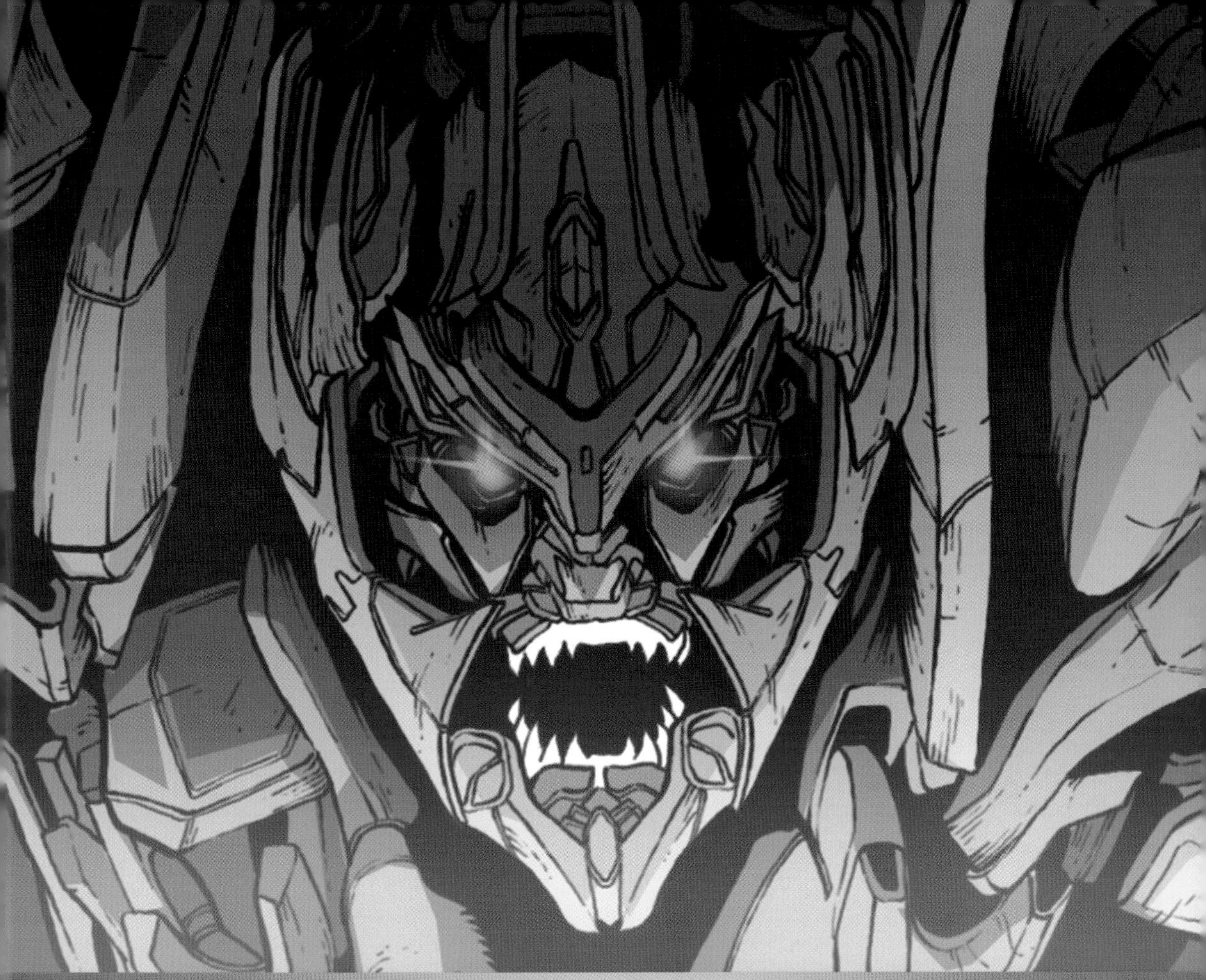

TRANSFORMERS: REVENGE OF THE FALLEN
ISSUE NUMBER TWO (OF FOUR)

WRITTEN BY: **SIMON FURMAN**
PENCILS BY: **JON DAVIS-HUNT**
COLORS BY: **KRIS CARTER**
LETTERS BY: **CHRIS MOWRY**
EDITS BY: **DENTON J. TIPTON**
ADAPTED FROM THE SCREENPLAY BY: **ROBERTO ORCI, ALEX KURTZMAN, AND EHREN KRUGER**

Special thanks to Hasbro's Aaron Archer, Michael Kelly, Amie Lozanzki, Va Roca, Ed Lane, Michael Provost, Erin Hillman, Samantha Lomow, and Michael Verecchia for their invaluable assistance.

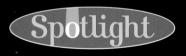

VISIT US AT
www.abdopublishing.com

Reinforced library bound edition published in 2010 by Spotlight, a division of the ABDO Group, 8000 West 78th Street, Edina, Minnesota 55439. Published by agreement with IDW Publishing. www.idwpublishing.com

Printed in the United States of America, Melrose Park, Illinois.
102009
012010

 PRINTED ON RECYCLED PAPER

Library of Congress Cataloging-in-Publication Data

Furman, Simon.
 Transformers : revenge of the fallen / written by Simon Furman ; pencils by Jon Davis-Hunt colors by Kris Carter and Josh Perez ; letters by Chris Mowry ; adapted from the screenplay by Roberto Orci, Alex Kurtzman, and Ehren Kruger.
     v. cm.
 ISBN 978-1-59961-726-8 (vol. 1) -- ISBN 978-1-59961-727-5 (vol. 2)
 ISBN 978-1-59961-728-2 (vol. 3) -- ISBN 978-1-59961-729-9 (vol. 4)
 1. Graphic novels. I. Davis-Hunt, Jon. II. Orci, Roberto. III. Kurtzman, Alex. IV. Kruger, Ehren, 1972- V. Transformers, revenge of the fallen (Motion picture) VI. Title.
 PZ7.7.F87Tr 2010
 741.5'973--dc22
                              2009037024

All Spotlight books have reinforced library bindings and are manufactured in the United States of America.

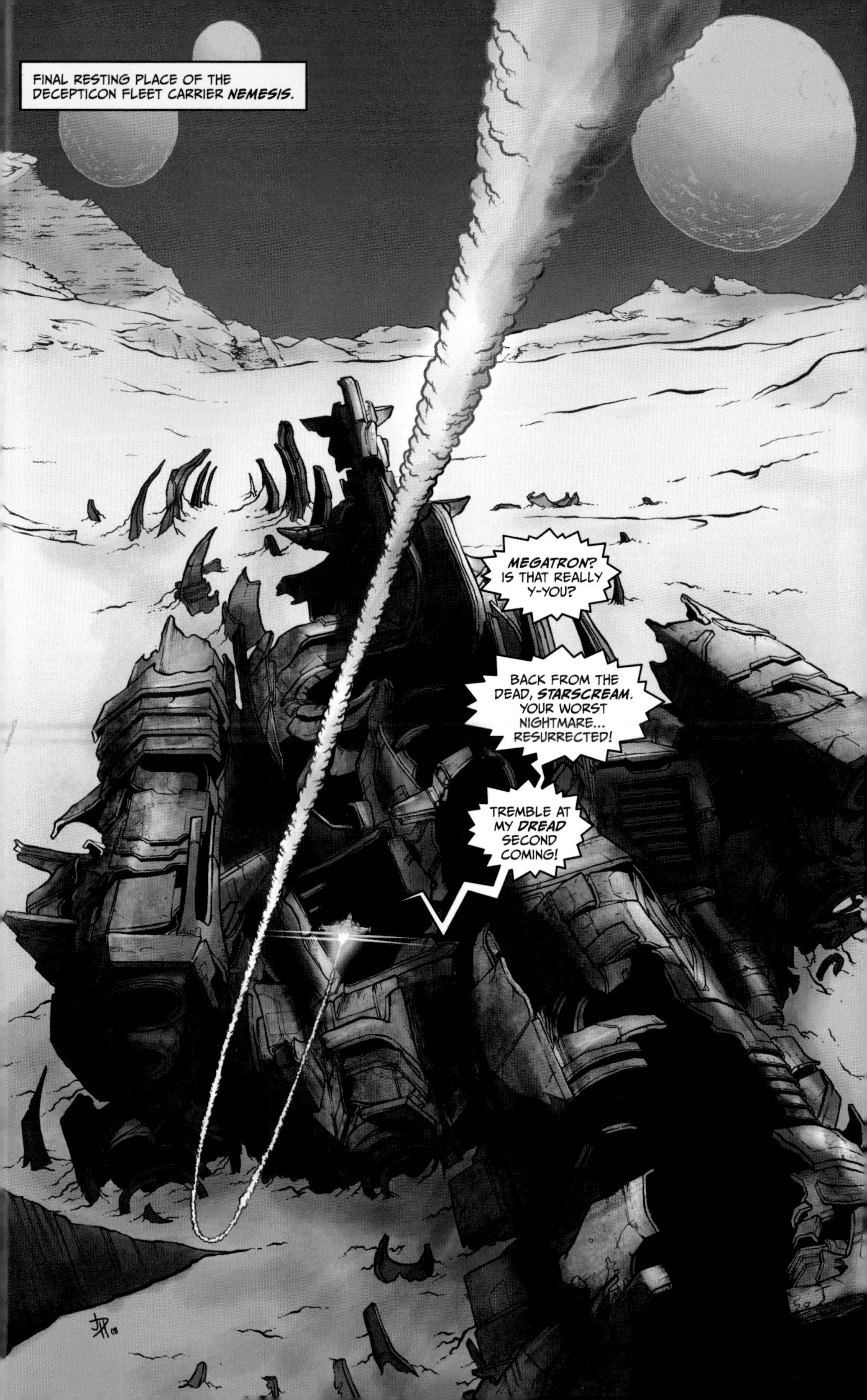
FINAL RESTING PLACE OF THE DECEPTICON FLEET CARRIER NEMESIS.
MEGATRON? IS THAT REALLY Y-YOU?
BACK FROM THE DEAD, STARSCREAM. YOUR WORST NIGHTMARE... RESURRECTED!
TREMBLE AT MY DREAD SECOND COMING!

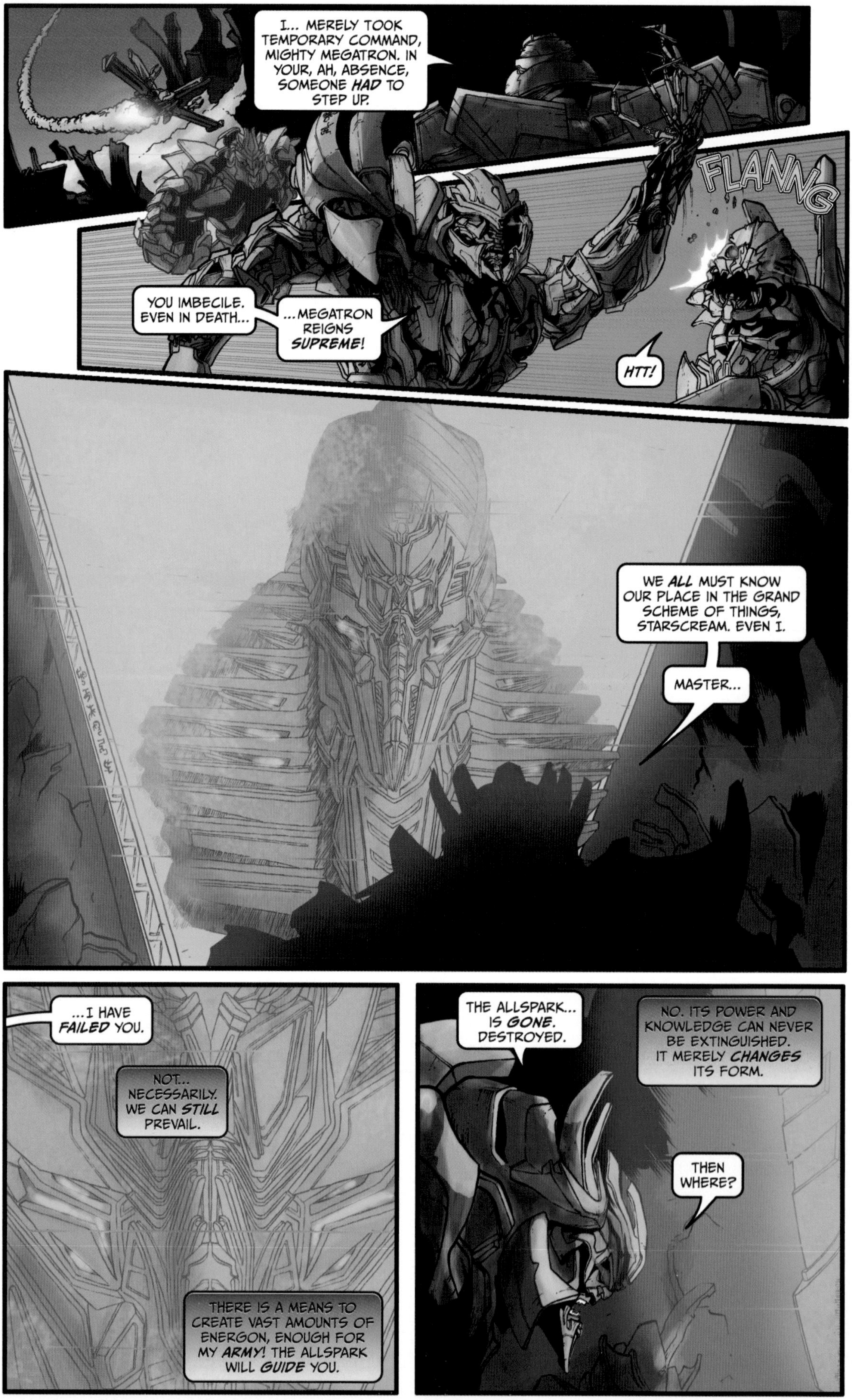

I... MERELY TOOK TEMPORARY COMMAND, MIGHTY MEGATRON. IN YOUR, AH, ABSENCE, SOMEONE HAD TO STEP UP.
FLANNG
YOU IMBECILE. EVEN IN DEATH...
...MEGATRON REIGNS SUPREME!
HTT!
WE ALL MUST KNOW OUR PLACE IN THE GRAND SCHEME OF THINGS, STARSCREAM. EVEN I.
MASTER...
...I HAVE FAILED YOU.
NOT... NECESSARILY. WE CAN STILL PREVAIL.
THERE IS A MEANS TO CREATE VAST AMOUNTS OF ENERGON, ENOUGH FOR MY ARMY! THE ALLSPARK WILL GUIDE YOU.
THE ALLSPARK... IS GONE. DESTROYED.
NO. ITS POWER AND KNOWLEDGE CAN NEVER BE EXTINGUISHED. IT MERELY CHANGES ITS FORM.
THEN WHERE?

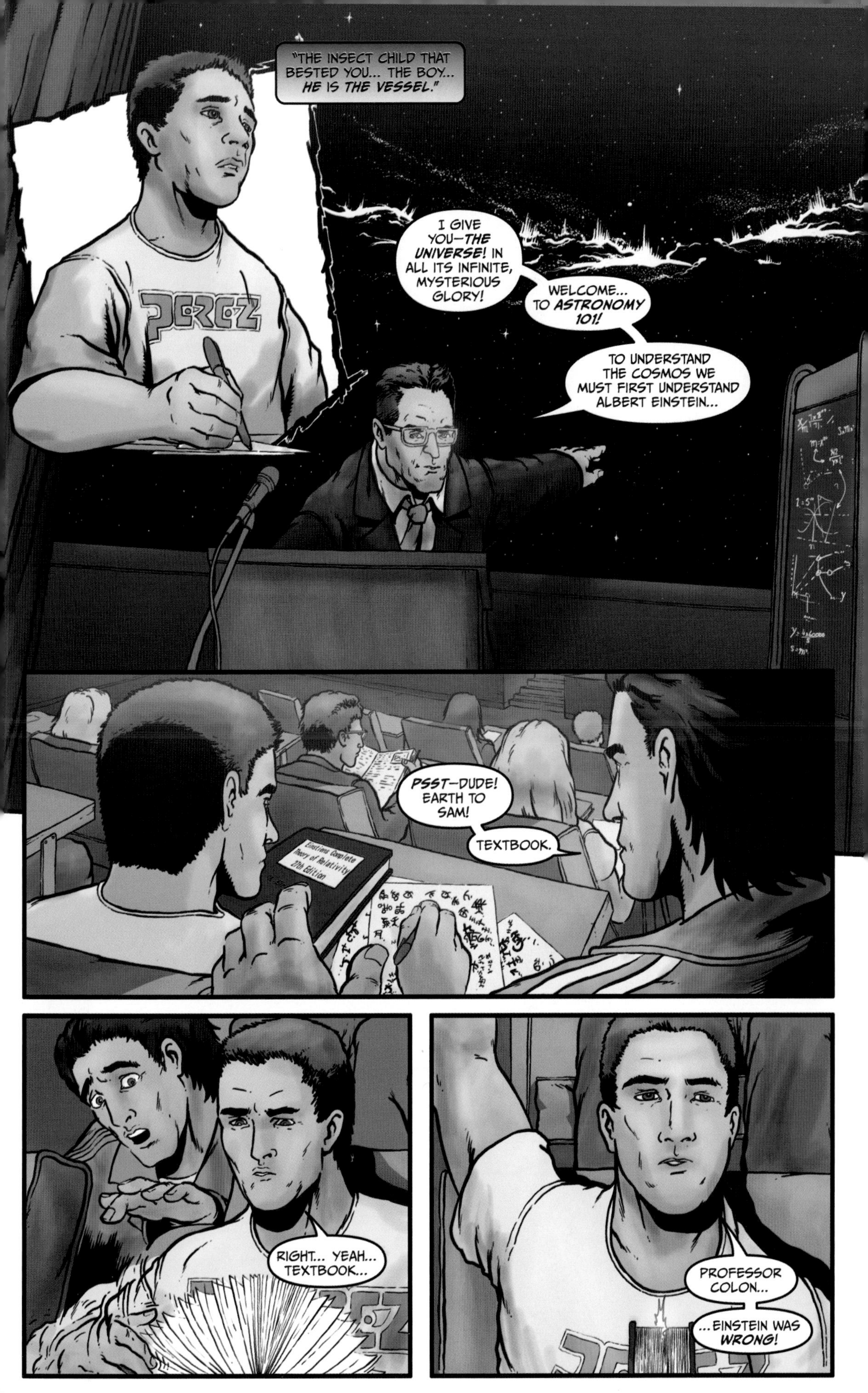
"THE INSECT CHILD THAT BESTED YOU... THE BOY... *HE* IS *THE VESSEL*."
I GIVE YOU—*THE UNIVERSE!* IN ALL ITS INFINITE, MYSTERIOUS GLORY!
WELCOME... TO *ASTRONOMY 101!*
TO UNDERSTAND THE COSMOS WE MUST FIRST UNDERSTAND ALBERT EINSTEIN...
PSST—DUDE! EARTH TO SAM!
TEXTBOOK.
Einstiens Complete Theory of Relativity 27th Edition
RIGHT... YEAH... TEXTBOOK...
PROFESSOR COLON...
...EINSTEIN WAS *WRONG!*

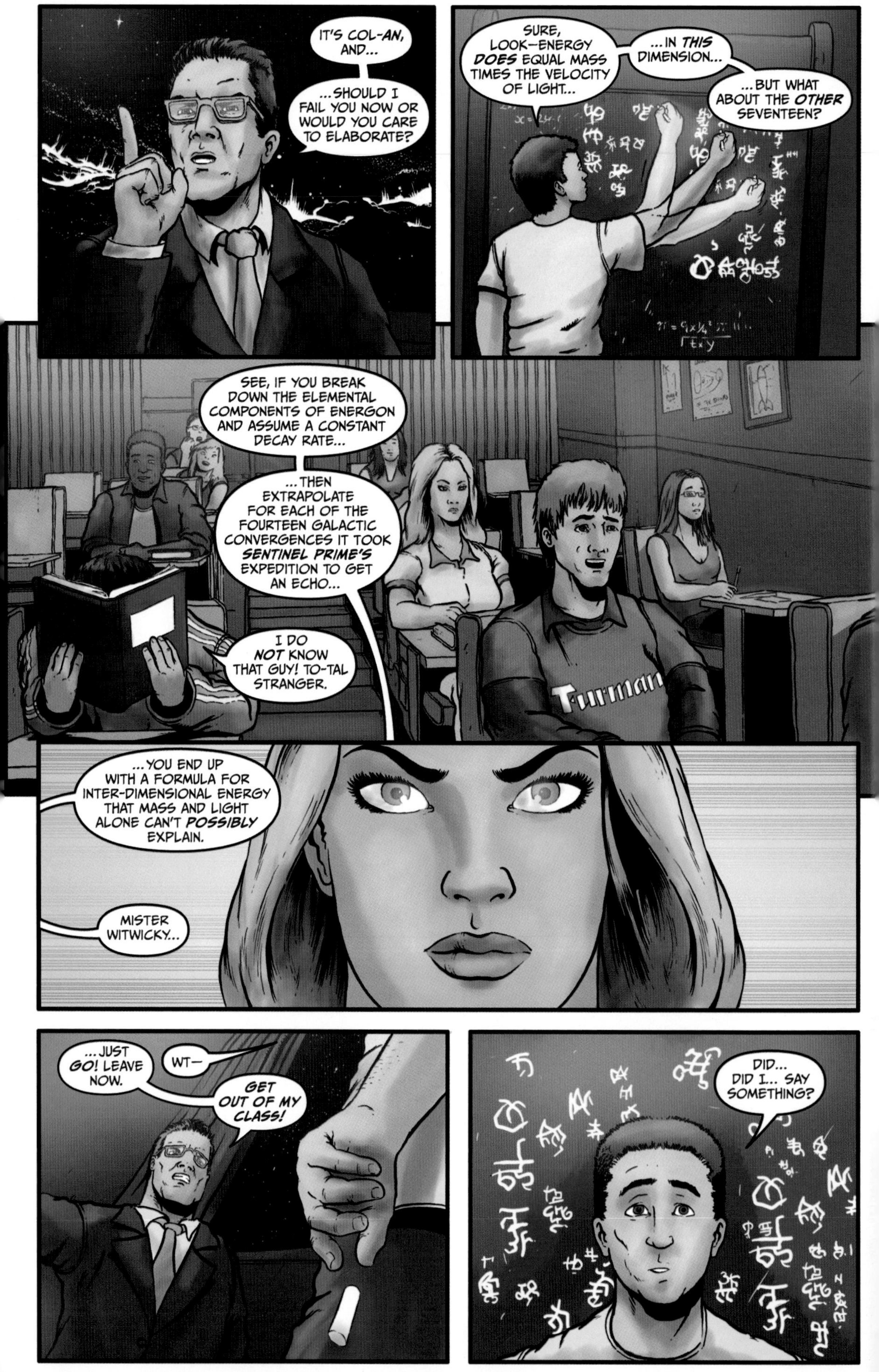
IT'S COL-AN, AND...
...SHOULD I FAIL YOU NOW OR WOULD YOU CARE TO ELABORATE?
SURE, LOOK—ENERGY DOES EQUAL MASS TIMES THE VELOCITY OF LIGHT...
...IN THIS DIMENSION...
...BUT WHAT ABOUT THE OTHER SEVENTEEN?
SEE, IF YOU BREAK DOWN THE ELEMENTAL COMPONENTS OF ENERGON AND ASSUME A CONSTANT DECAY RATE...
...THEN EXTRAPOLATE FOR EACH OF THE FOURTEEN GALACTIC CONVERGENCES IT TOOK SENTINEL PRIME'S EXPEDITION TO GET AN ECHO...
I DO NOT KNOW THAT GUY! TO-TAL STRANGER.
Turman
...YOU END UP WITH A FORMULA FOR INTER-DIMENSIONAL ENERGY THAT MASS AND LIGHT ALONE CAN'T POSSIBLY EXPLAIN.
MISTER WITWICKY...
...JUST GO! LEAVE NOW.
WT—
GET OUT OF MY CLASS!
DID... DID I... SAY SOMETHING?

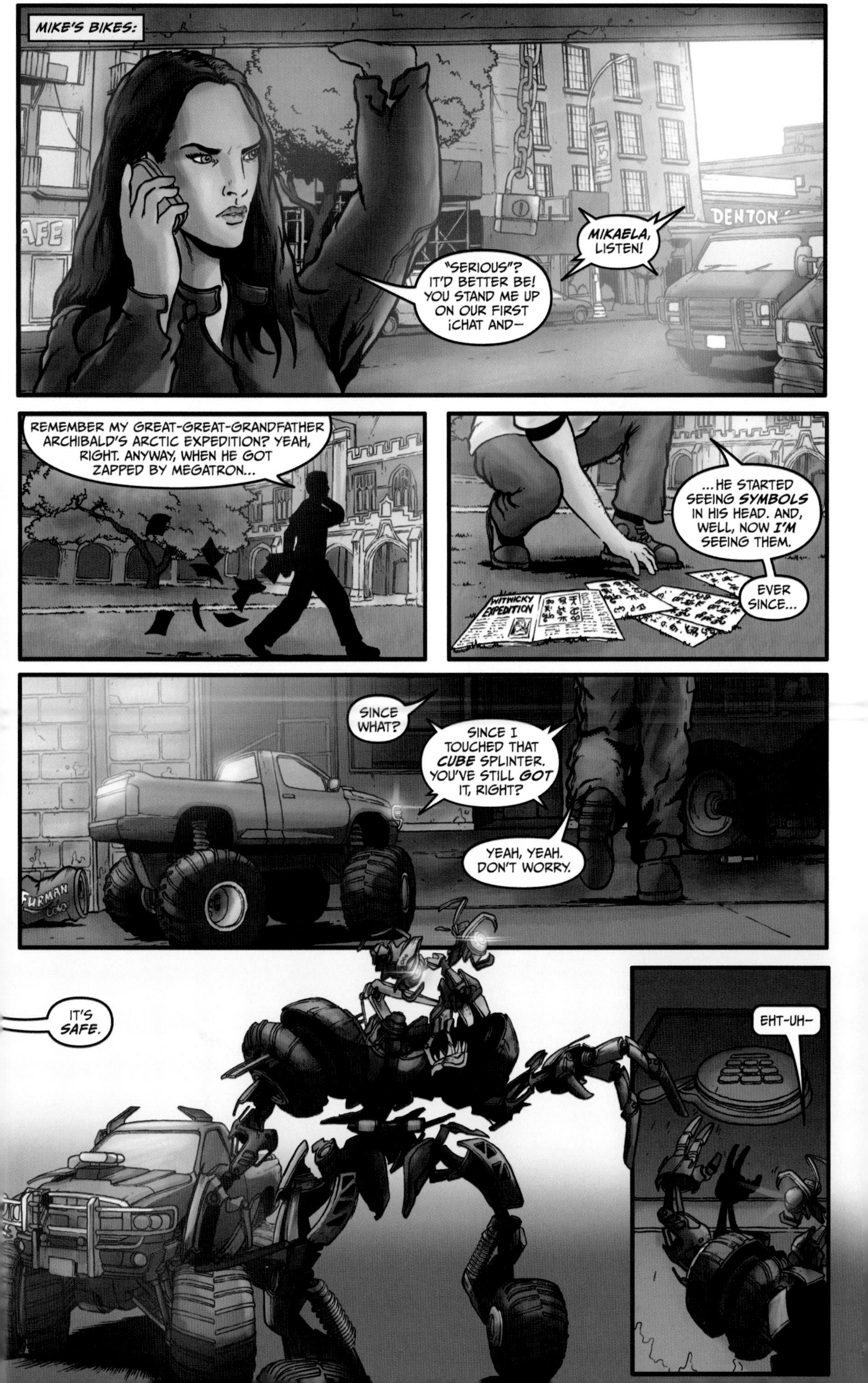
MIKE'S BIKES:
DENTON'S
"SERIOUS"? IT'D BETTER BE! YOU STAND ME UP ON OUR FIRST iCHAT AND—
MIKAELA, LISTEN!
REMEMBER MY GREAT-GREAT-GRANDFATHER ARCHIBALD'S ARCTIC EXPEDITION? YEAH, RIGHT. ANYWAY, WHEN HE GOT ZAPPED BY MEGATRON...
...HE STARTED SEEING SYMBOLS IN HIS HEAD. AND, WELL, NOW I'M SEEING THEM.
EVER SINCE...
WITWICKY EXPEDITION
SINCE WHAT?
SINCE I TOUCHED THAT CUBE SPLINTER. YOU'VE STILL GOT IT, RIGHT?
YEAH, YEAH. DON'T WORRY.
FURMAN
IT'S SAFE.
EHT-UH—

OW!

SNAP

KLATTER

ACK!

YOU...

...START TALKING. NOW!

MIKAELA? WHAT *WAS* THAT? ARE YOU OKAY?

JUST SIT TIGHT, SAM, I'M COMING OUT.

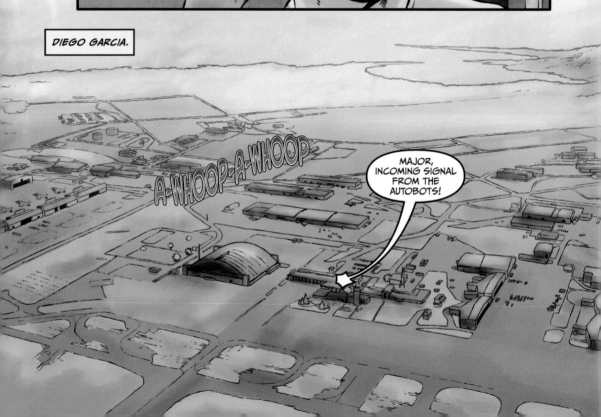

DIEGO GARCIA.

A-WHOOP-A-WHOOP

MAJOR, INCOMING SIGNAL FROM THE AUTOBOTS!

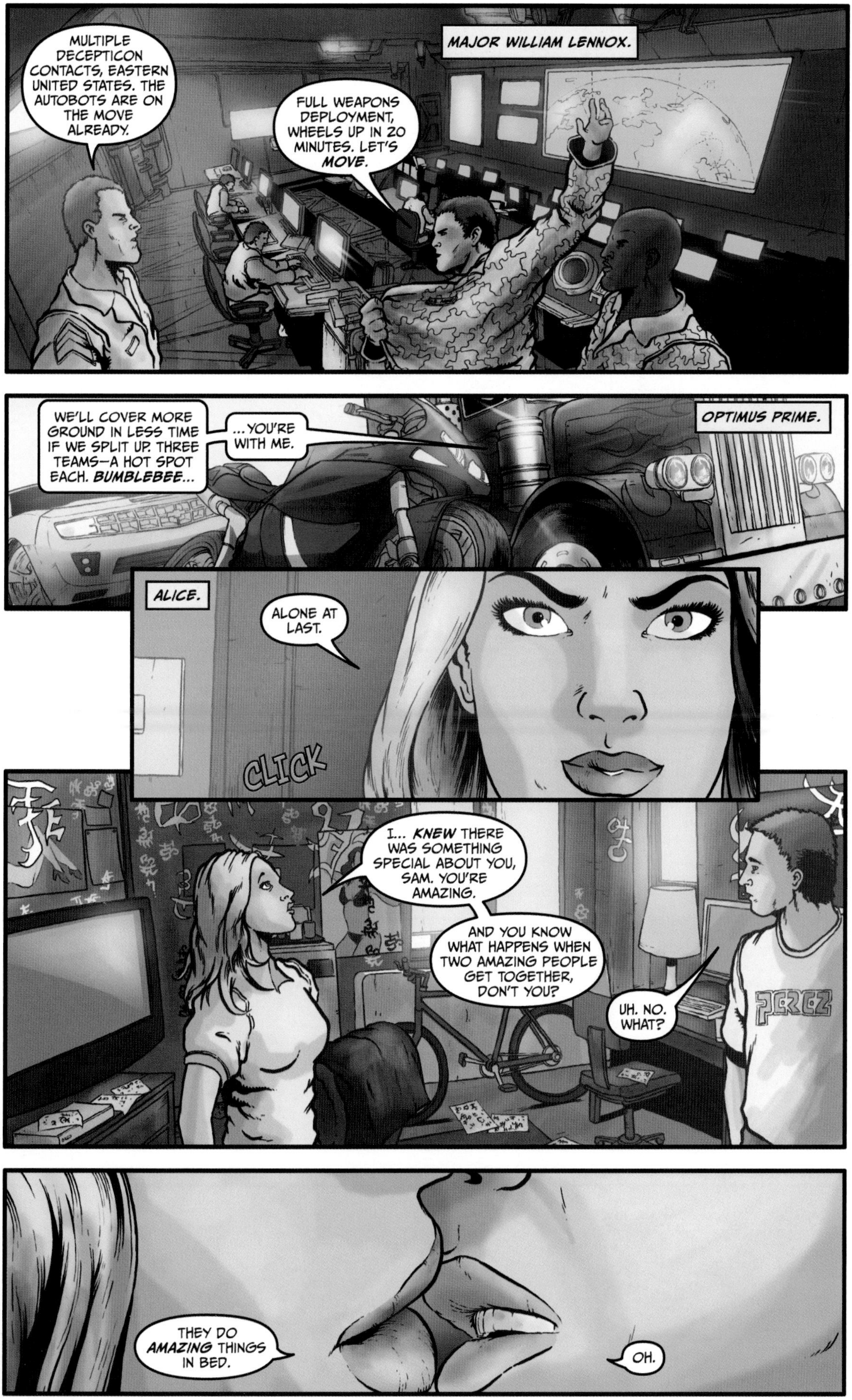
MAJOR WILLIAM LENNOX.
MULTIPLE DECEPTICON CONTACTS, EASTERN UNITED STATES. THE AUTOBOTS ARE ON THE MOVE ALREADY.
FULL WEAPONS DEPLOYMENT, WHEELS UP IN 20 MINUTES. LET'S MOVE.
OPTIMUS PRIME.
WE'LL COVER MORE GROUND IN LESS TIME IF WE SPLIT UP. THREE TEAMS—A HOT SPOT EACH. BUMBLEBEE...
...YOU'RE WITH ME.
ALICE.
ALONE AT LAST.
CLICK
I... KNEW THERE WAS SOMETHING SPECIAL ABOUT YOU, SAM. YOU'RE AMAZING.
AND YOU KNOW WHAT HAPPENS WHEN TWO AMAZING PEOPLE GET TOGETHER, DON'T YOU?
UH. NO. WHAT?
THEY DO AMAZING THINGS IN BED.
OH.

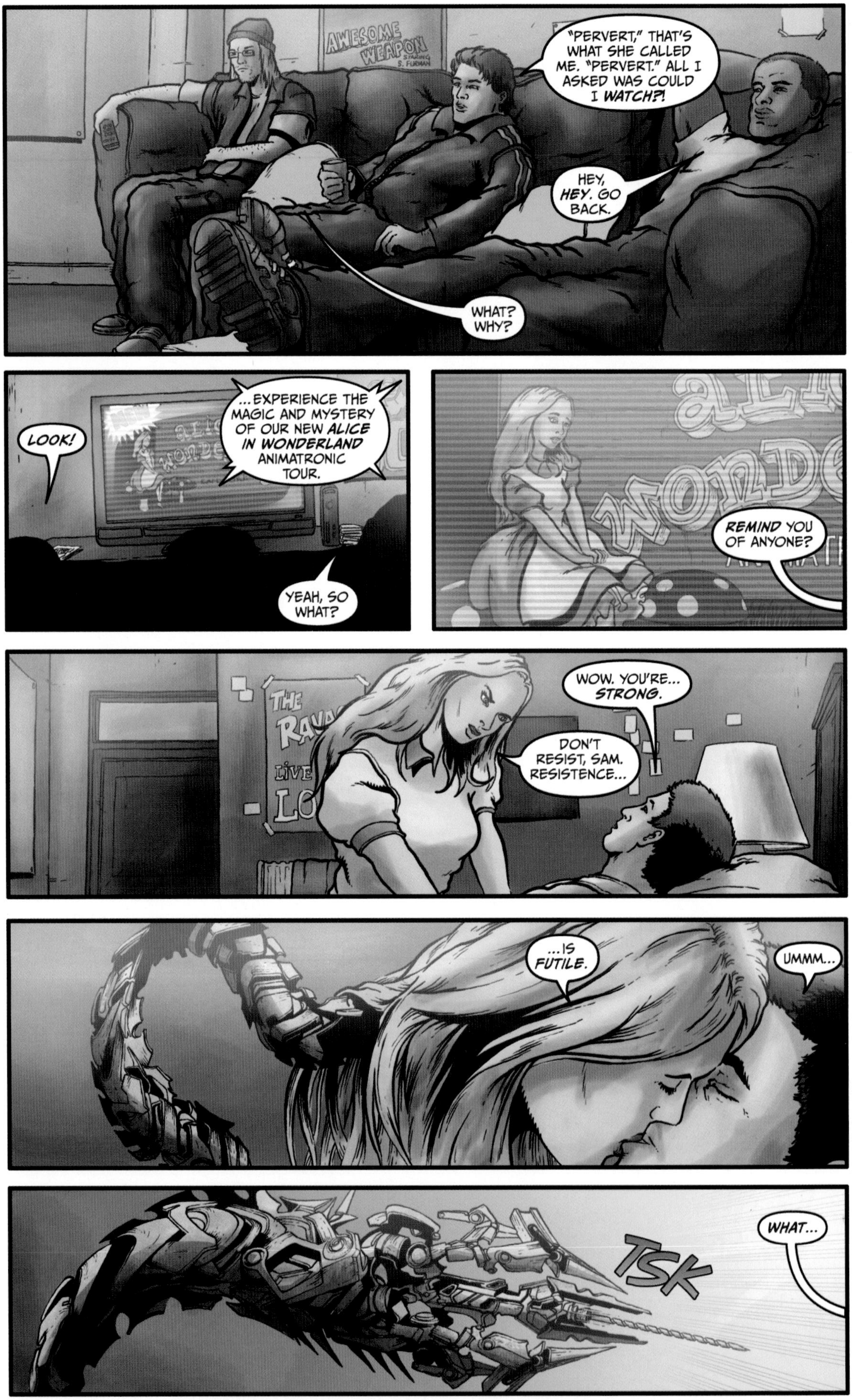
AWESOME WEAPON STARRING S. FURMAN
"PERVERT," THAT'S WHAT SHE CALLED ME. "PERVERT." ALL I ASKED WAS COULD I WATCH?!
HEY, HEY. GO BACK.
WHAT? WHY?
LOOK!
...EXPERIENCE THE MAGIC AND MYSTERY OF OUR NEW ALICE IN WONDERLAND ANIMATRONIC TOUR.
YEAH, SO WHAT?
REMIND YOU OF ANYONE?
WOW. YOU'RE... STRONG.
DON'T RESIST, SAM. RESISTENCE...
...IS FUTILE.
UMMM...
TSK
WHAT...

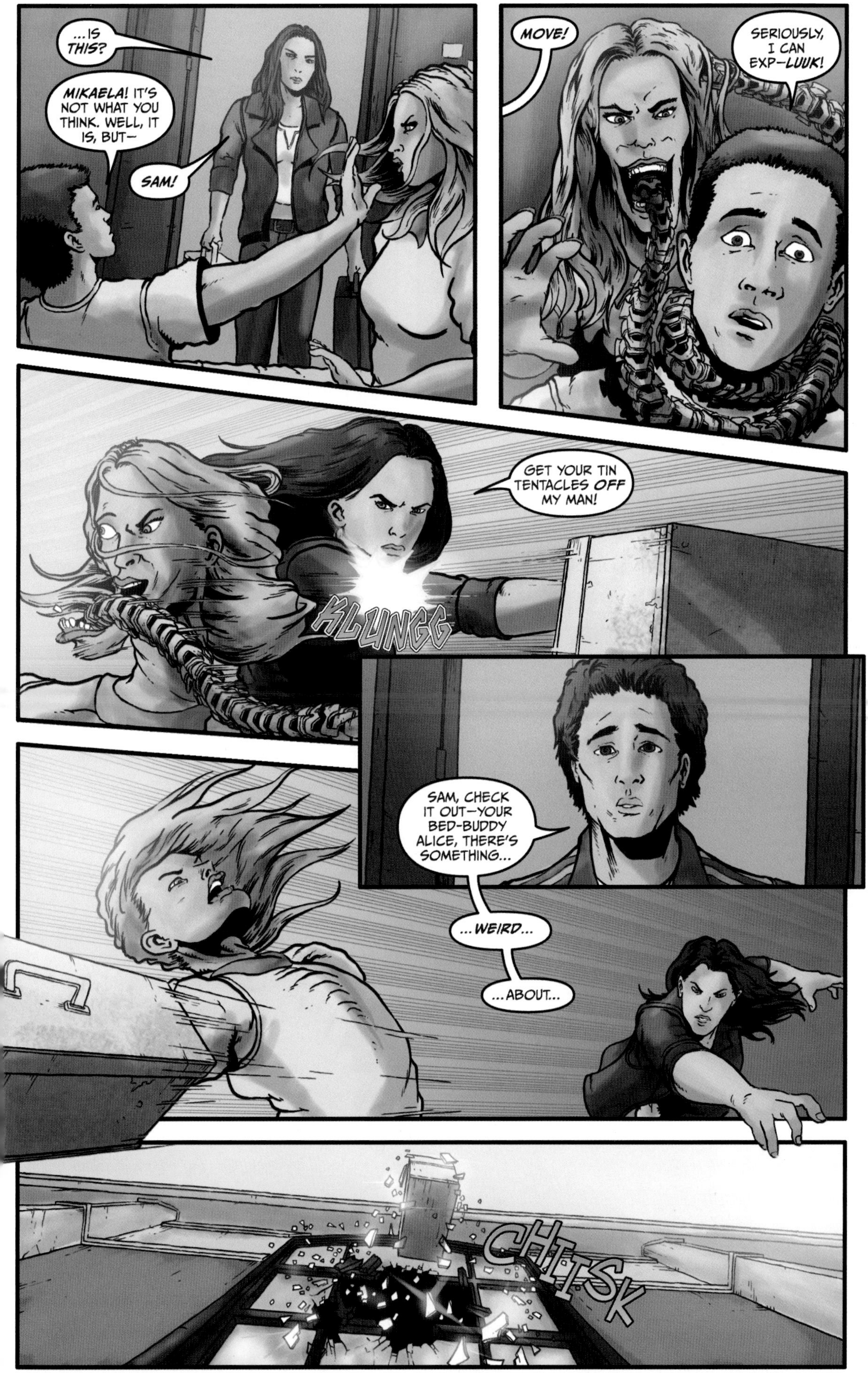
...IS THIS?
MIKAELA! IT'S NOT WHAT YOU THINK. WELL, IT IS, BUT—
SAM!
MOVE!
SERIOUSLY, I CAN EXP—LUUK!
GET YOUR TIN TENTACLES OFF MY MAN!
KLUNGG
SAM, CHECK IT OUT—YOUR BED-BUDDY ALICE, THERE'S SOMETHING...
...WEIRD...
...ABOUT...
CHISK

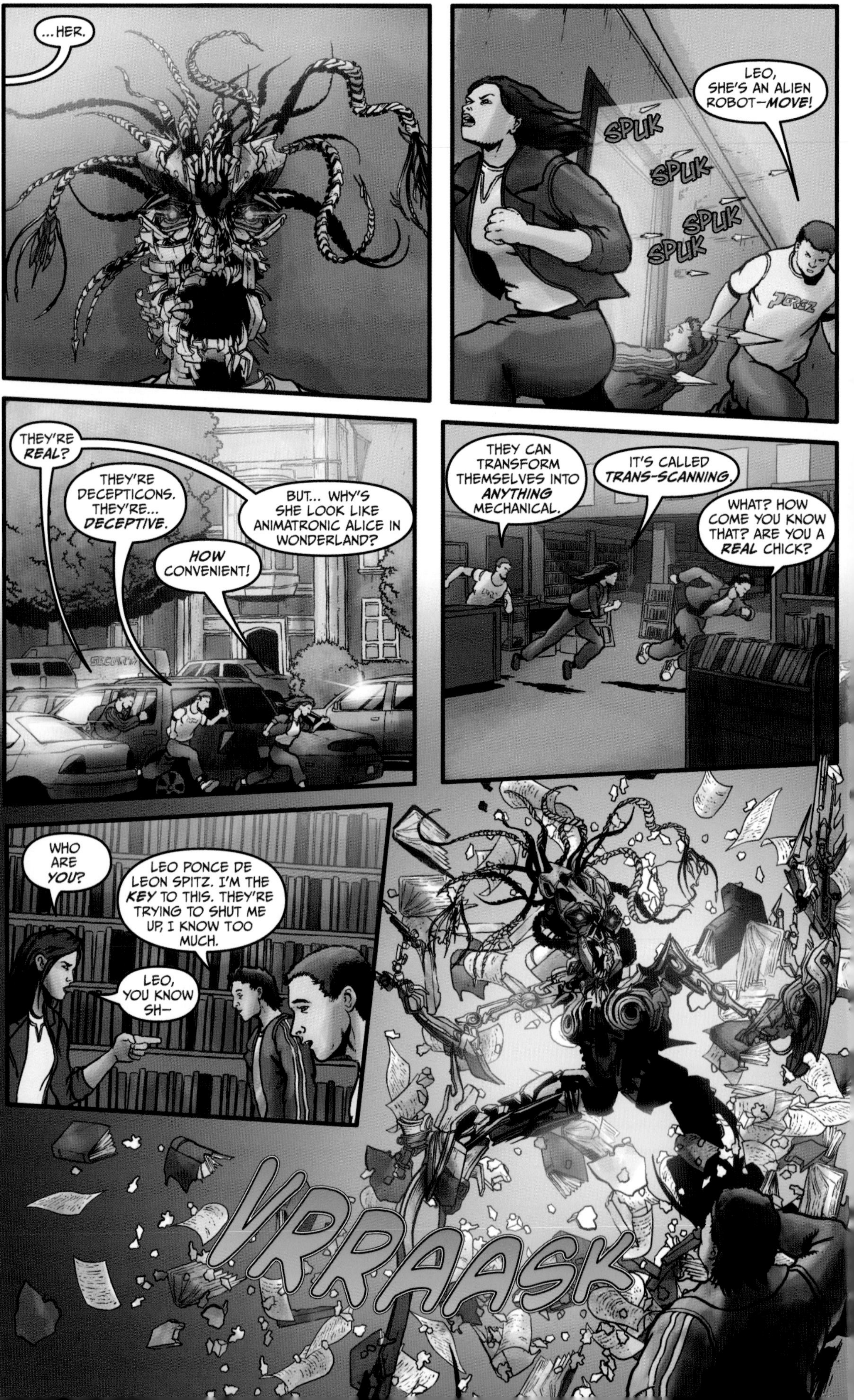
...HER.
LEO, SHE'S AN ALIEN ROBOT—MOVE!
SPUK
SPUK
SPUK
SPUK
THEY'RE REAL?
THEY'RE DECEPTICONS. THEY'RE... DECEPTIVE.
BUT... WHY'S SHE LOOK LIKE ANIMATRONIC ALICE IN WONDERLAND?
HOW CONVENIENT!
THEY CAN TRANSFORM THEMSELVES INTO ANYTHING MECHANICAL.
IT'S CALLED TRANS-SCANNING.
WHAT? HOW COME YOU KNOW THAT? ARE YOU A REAL CHICK?
WHO ARE YOU?
LEO PONCE DE LEON SPITZ. I'M THE KEY TO THIS. THEY'RE TRYING TO SHUT ME UP, I KNOW TOO MUCH.
LEO, YOU KNOW SH—
VRRAASK

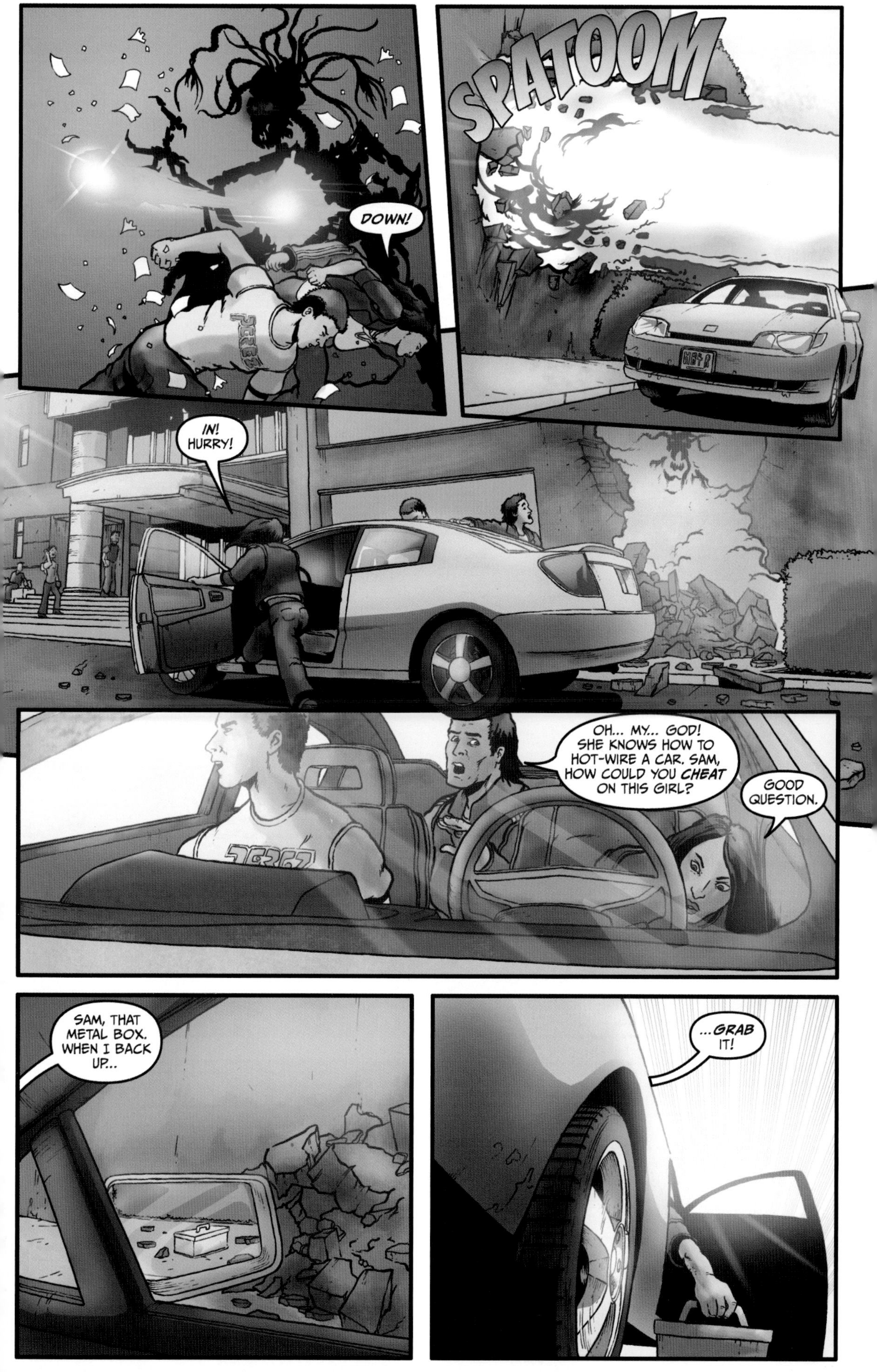
DOWN!
SPATOOM
IN! HURRY!
OH... MY... GOD! SHE KNOWS HOW TO HOT-WIRE A CAR. SAM, HOW COULD YOU CHEAT ON THIS GIRL?
GOOD QUESTION.
SAM, THAT METAL BOX. WHEN I BACK UP...
...GRAB IT!

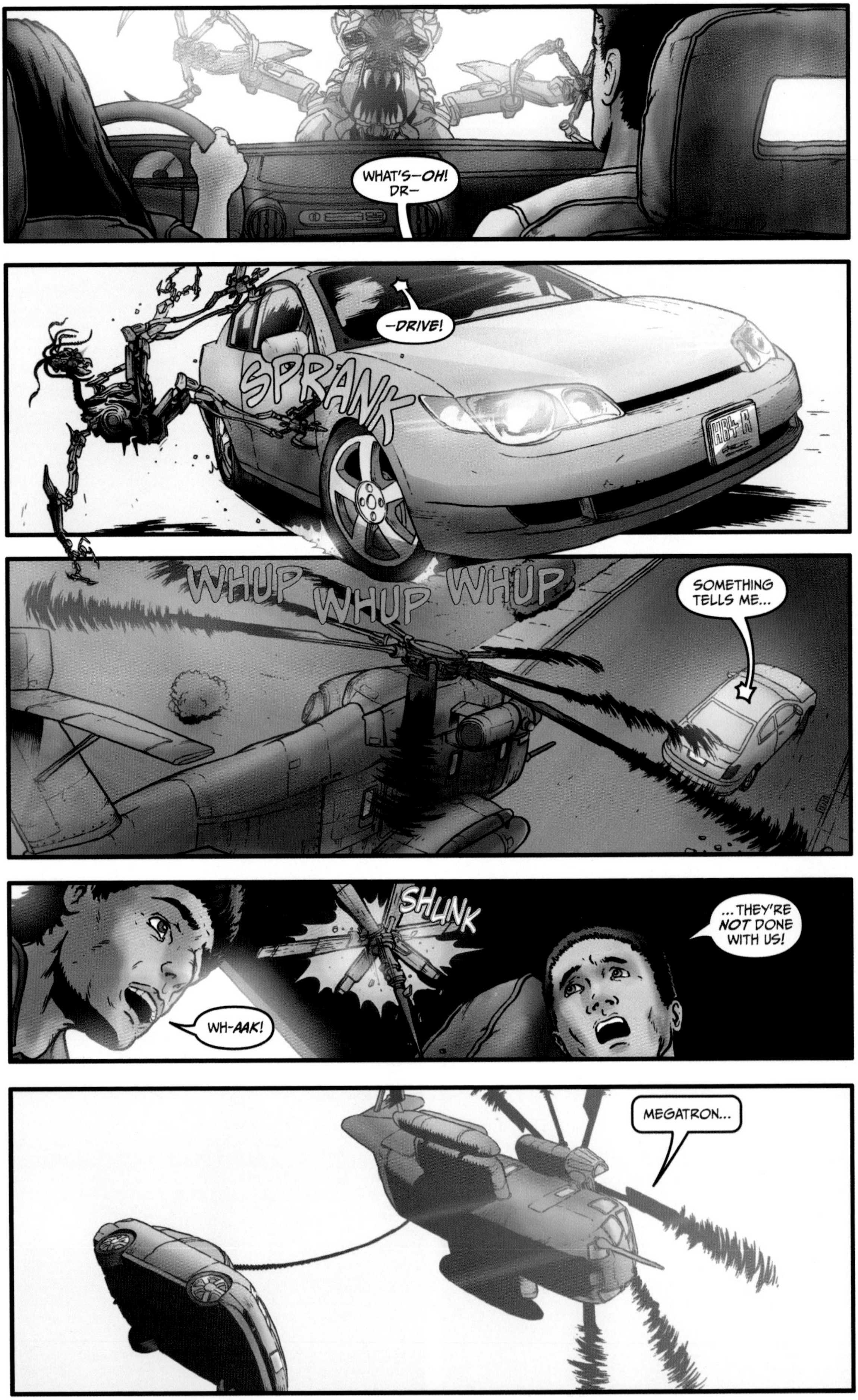
WHAT'S—OH! DR—
—DRIVE!
SPRANK
WHUP WHUP WHUP
SOMETHING TELLS ME...
SHUNK
...THEY'RE NOT DONE WITH US!
WH-AAK!
MEGATRON...

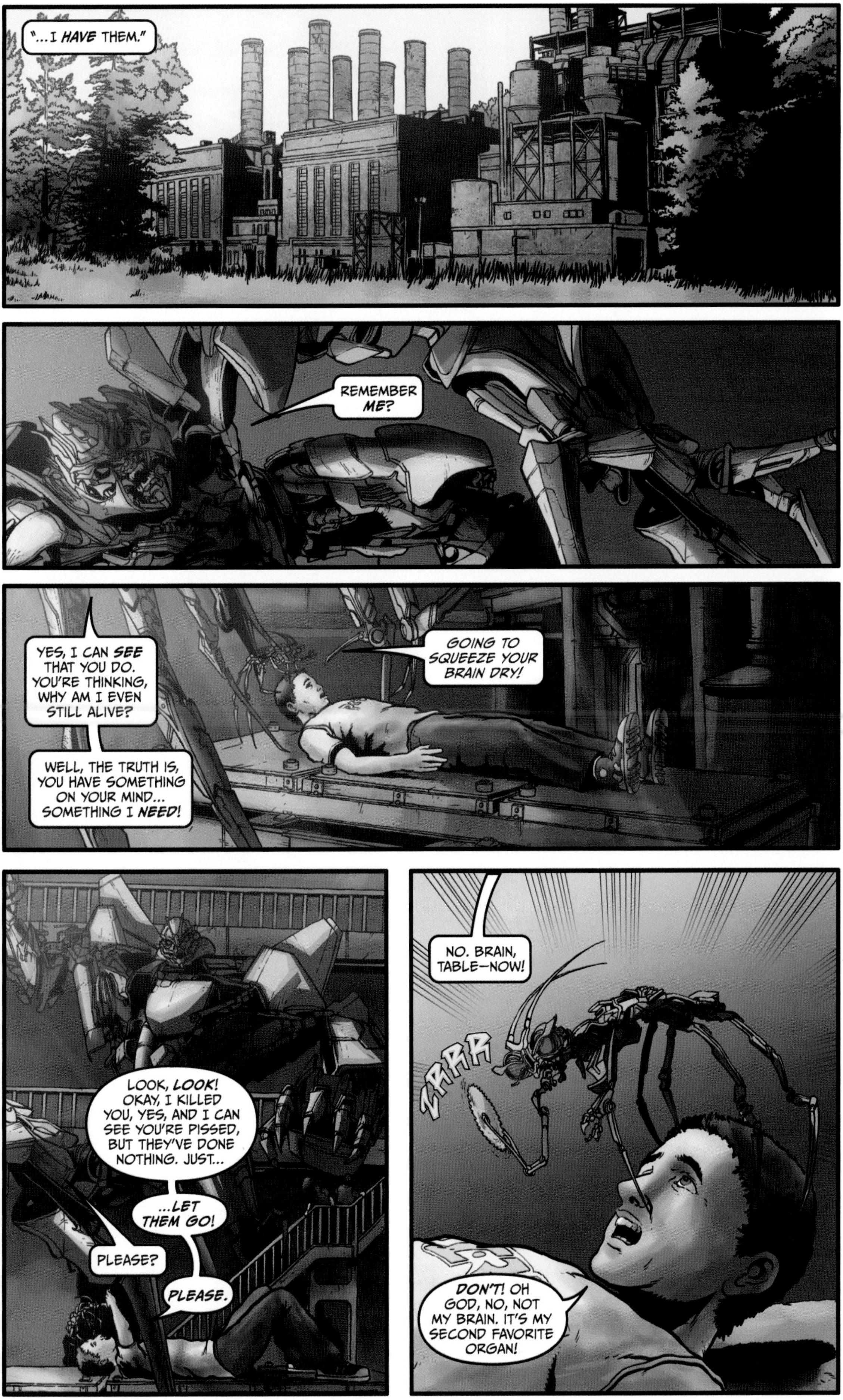
"...I HAVE THEM."
REMEMBER ME?
YES, I CAN SEE THAT YOU DO. YOU'RE THINKING, WHY AM I EVEN STILL ALIVE?
GOING TO SQUEEZE YOUR BRAIN DRY!
WELL, THE TRUTH IS, YOU HAVE SOMETHING ON YOUR MIND... SOMETHING I NEED!
LOOK, LOOK! OKAY, I KILLED YOU, YES, AND I CAN SEE YOU'RE PISSED, BUT THEY'VE DONE NOTHING. JUST...
...LET THEM GO!
PLEASE?
PLEASE.
NO. BRAIN, TABLE—NOW!
ZRRR
DON'T! OH GOD, NO, NOT MY BRAIN. IT'S MY SECOND FAVORITE ORGAN!

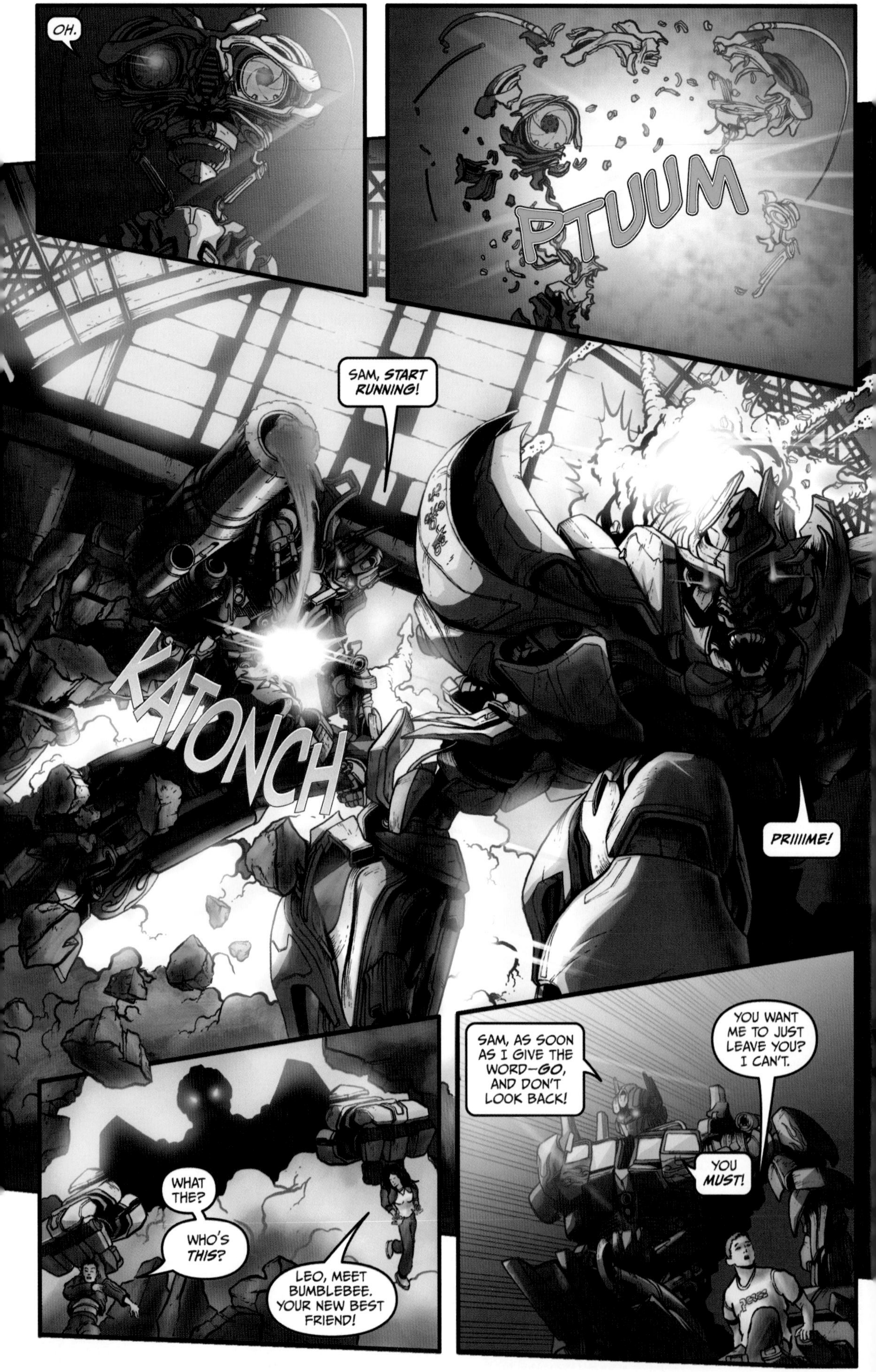
OH.
PTUUM
SAM, START RUNNING!
KATONCH
PRIIIIME!
WHAT THE?
WHO'S THIS?
LEO, MEET BUMBLEBEE. YOUR NEW BEST FRIEND!
SAM, AS SOON AS I GIVE THE WORD—GO, AND DON'T LOOK BACK!
YOU WANT ME TO JUST LEAVE YOU? I CAN'T.
YOU MUST!

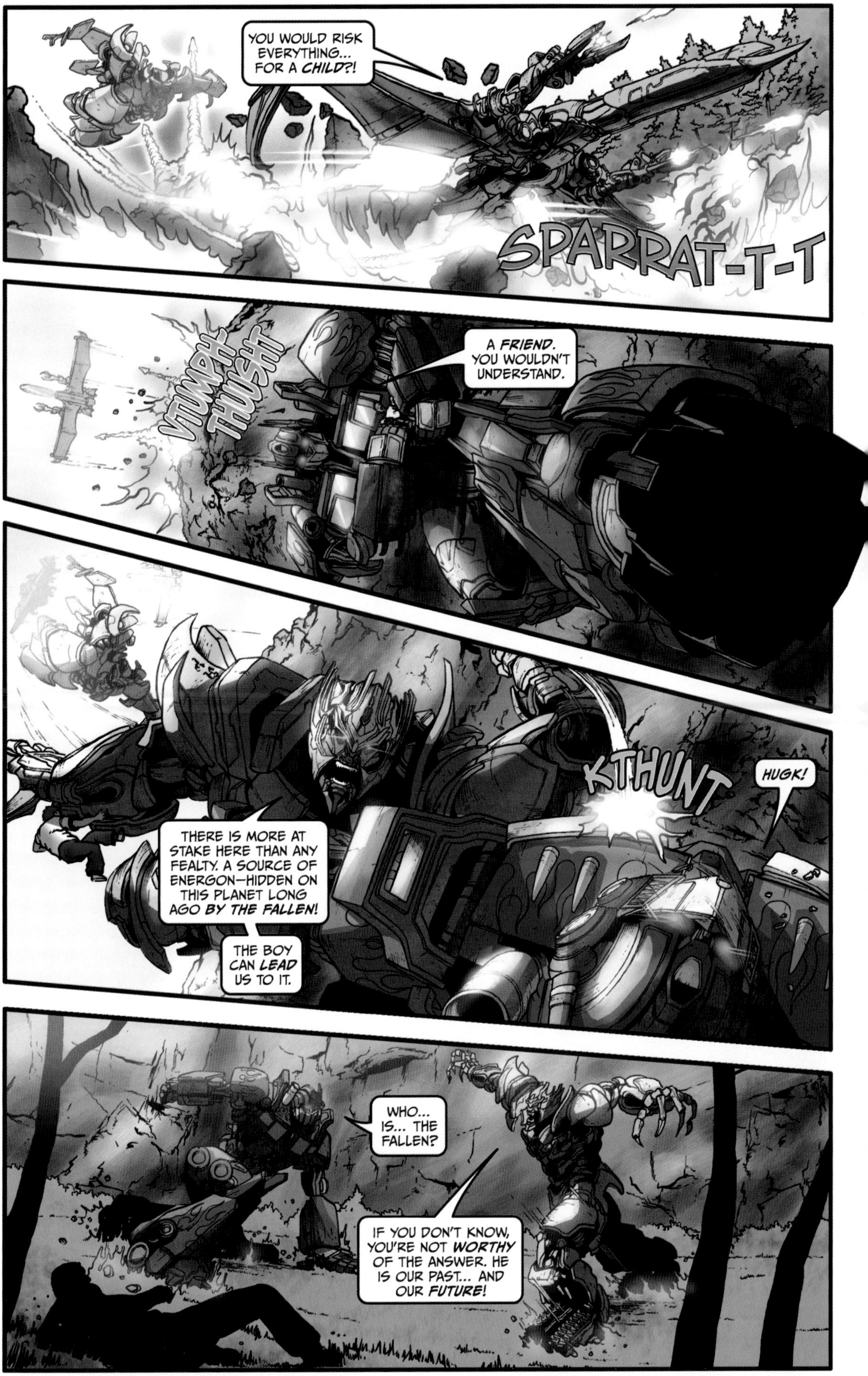

YOU WOULD RISK EVERYTHING... FOR A *CHILD*?!
SPARRAT-T-T
VTUMPH THUSHT
A *FRIEND*. YOU WOULDN'T UNDERSTAND.
KTHUNT
HUGK!
THERE IS MORE AT STAKE HERE THAN ANY FEALTY. A SOURCE OF ENERGON—HIDDEN ON THIS PLANET LONG AGO *BY THE FALLEN*!
THE BOY CAN *LEAD* US TO IT.
WHO... IS... THE FALLEN?
IF YOU DON'T KNOW, YOU'RE NOT *WORTHY* OF THE ANSWER. HE IS OUR PAST... AND OUR *FUTURE*!

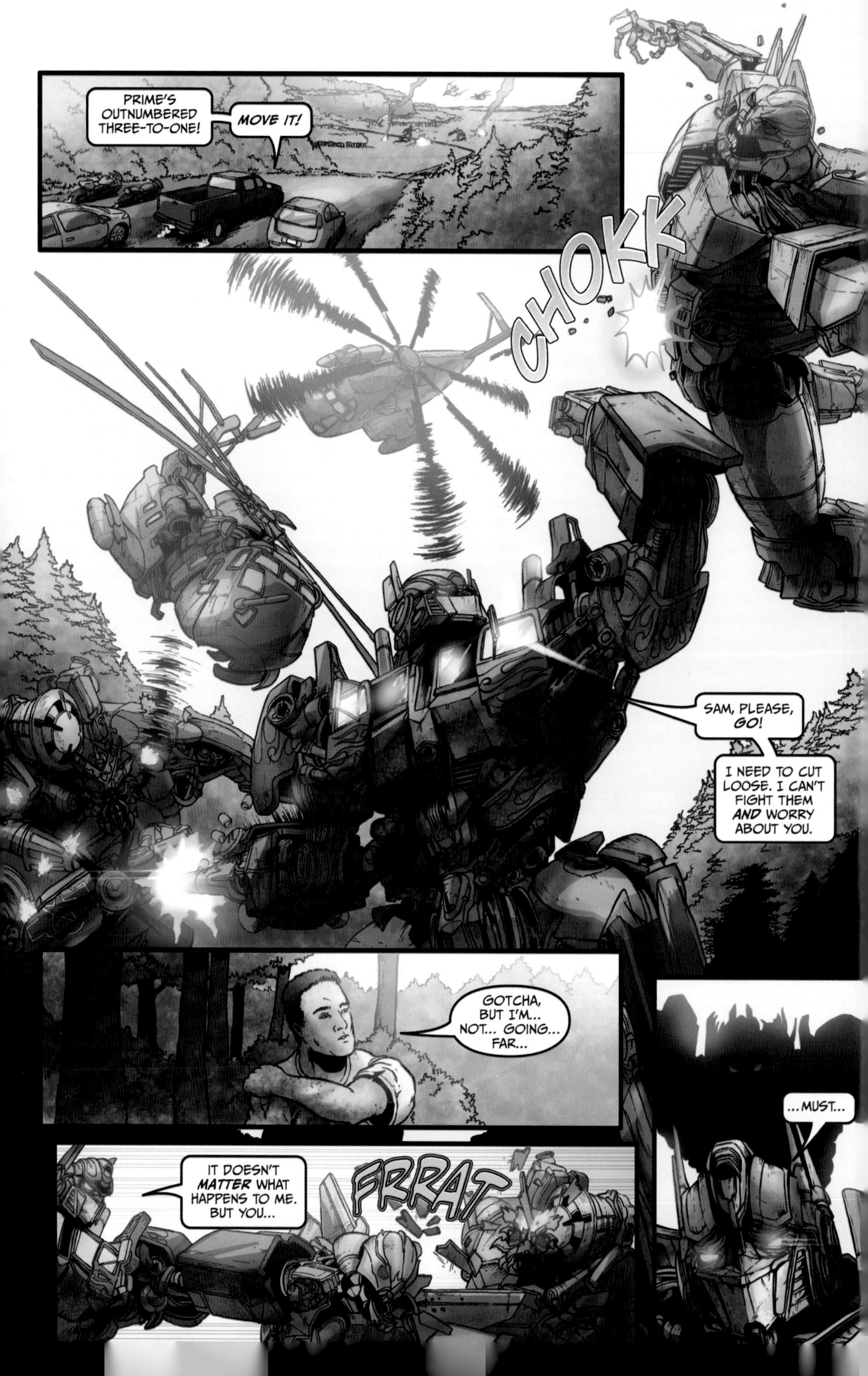
PRIME'S OUTNUMBERED THREE-TO-ONE!
MOVE IT!
CHOKK
SAM, PLEASE, GO!
I NEED TO CUT LOOSE. I CAN'T FIGHT THEM AND WORRY ABOUT YOU.
GOTCHA, BUT I'M... NOT... GOING... FAR...
IT DOESN'T MATTER WHAT HAPPENS TO ME. BUT YOU...
FRRAT
...MUST...

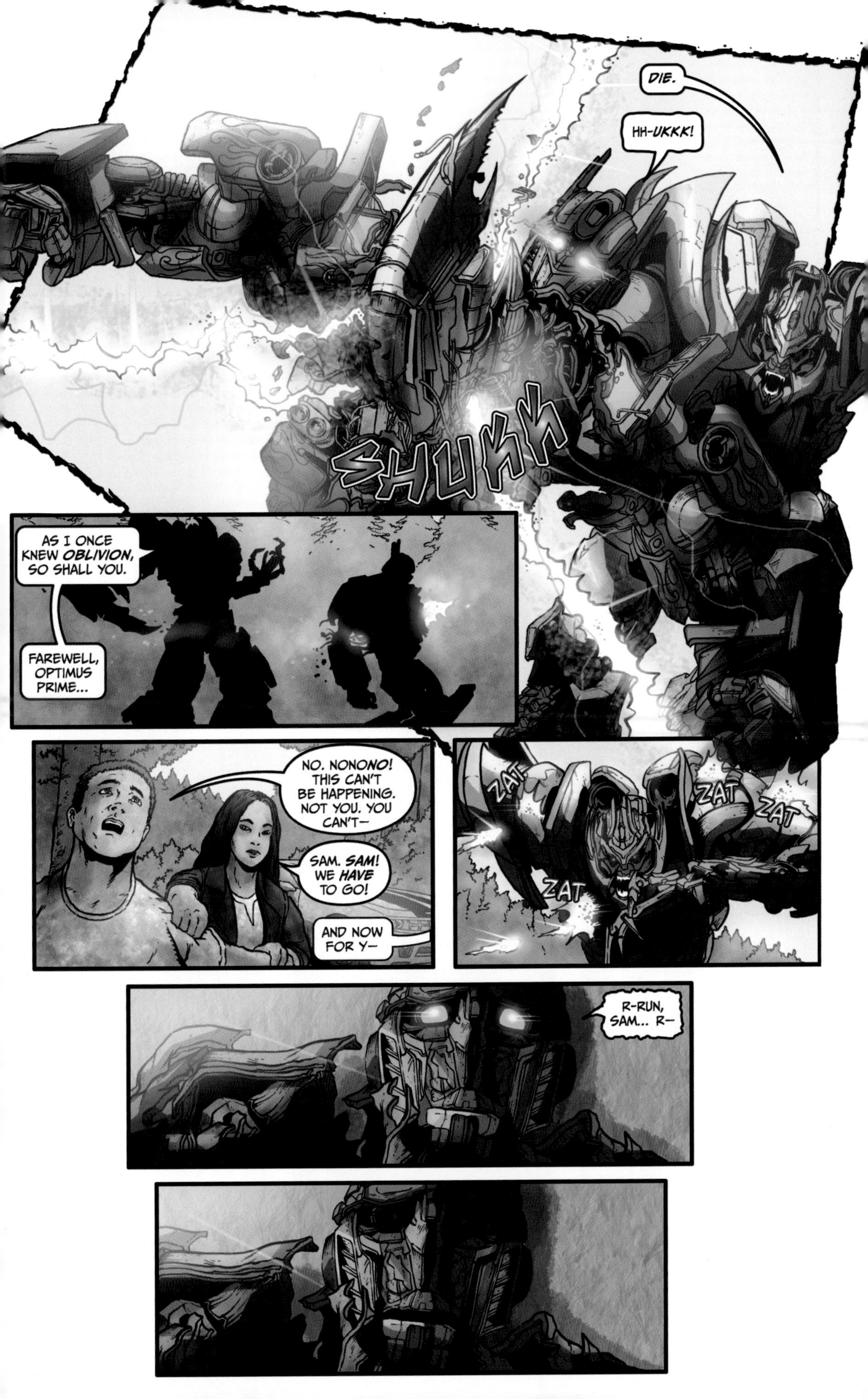

DIE.
HH-UKKK!
SHUKK
AS I ONCE KNEW OBLIVION, SO SHALL YOU.
FAREWELL, OPTIMUS PRIME...
NO. NONONO! THIS CAN'T BE HAPPENING. NOT YOU. YOU CAN'T—
SAM. SAM! WE HAVE TO GO!
AND NOW FOR Y—
ZAT
ZAT
ZAT
ZAT
R-RUN, SAM... R—

C'MON...
THERE'S NOTHING
MORE YOU CAN
DO, SAM.

MOVE
IT!

WHAPOOM

HURT
THEM.

PRIME?

HE'S...

...HE'S
NEARLY
GONE...

THE
BOY?

WE... LOST
HIM. HE'LL GO
TO GROUND.

TELL ME,
STARSCREAM...

"...WHERE CAN HE HIDE?"

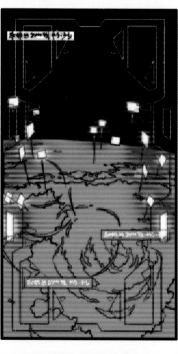

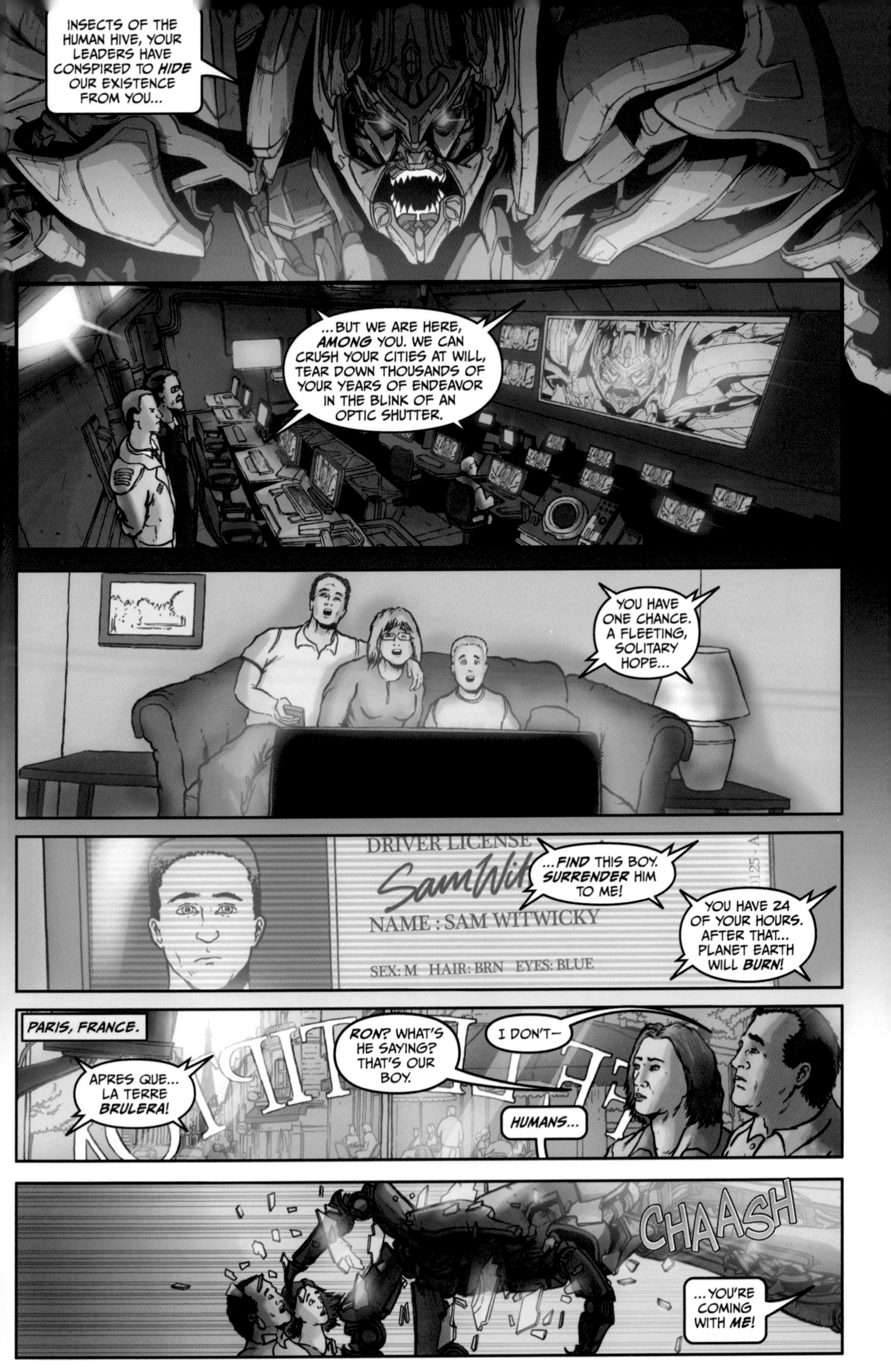
INSECTS OF THE HUMAN HIVE, YOUR LEADERS HAVE CONSPIRED TO *HIDE* OUR EXISTENCE FROM YOU...
...BUT WE ARE HERE, *AMONG* YOU. WE CAN CRUSH YOUR CITIES AT WILL, TEAR DOWN THOUSANDS OF YOUR YEARS OF ENDEAVOR IN THE BLINK OF AN OPTIC SHUTTER.
YOU HAVE ONE CHANCE. A FLEETING, SOLITARY HOPE...
DRIVER LICENSE
NAME : SAM WITWICKY
SEX: M HAIR: BRN EYES: BLUE
...*FIND* THIS BOY. *SURRENDER* HIM TO ME!
YOU HAVE 24 OF YOUR HOURS. AFTER THAT... PLANET EARTH WILL *BURN*!
PARIS, FRANCE.
APRES QUE... LA TERRE *BRULERA*!
RON? WHAT'S HE SAYING? THAT'S OUR BOY.
I DON'T—
HUMANS...
CHAASH
...YOU'RE COMING WITH *ME*!

LEMME SEE IF I HAVE THIS STRAIGHT...

...LENNOX IS *MAJOR* LENNOX NO MORE, THE AUTOBOTS HAVE BEEN STOOD DOWN, AND OPTIMUS PRIME MAY NOT LIVE...

...ALL BECAUSE OF *ME*.

DID I MISS ANYTHING?

ACTUALLY, YEAH. SEEMS YOU'RE *ALSO* PUBLIC ENEMY NO. 1. EVERYONE—AND I MEAN *EVERYONE*—IS LOOKING FOR YOU.

GREAT. I SHOULD JUST TURN MYSELF IN.

NO *WAY!* YOU THINK IF MEGATRON GETS WHAT HE WANTS HE'LL JUST LEAVE THE REST OF THE WORLD BE?

THERE'S *GOT* TO BE ANOTHER WAY!

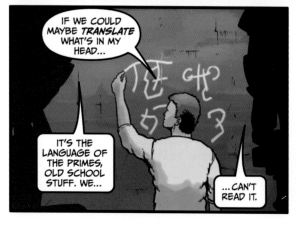

IF WE COULD MAYBE *TRANSLATE* WHAT'S IN MY HEAD...

IT'S THE LANGUAGE OF THE PRIMES, OLD SCHOOL STUFF. WE...

...CAN'T READ IT.

I... THINK I KNOW SOMEONE WHO *CAN*.

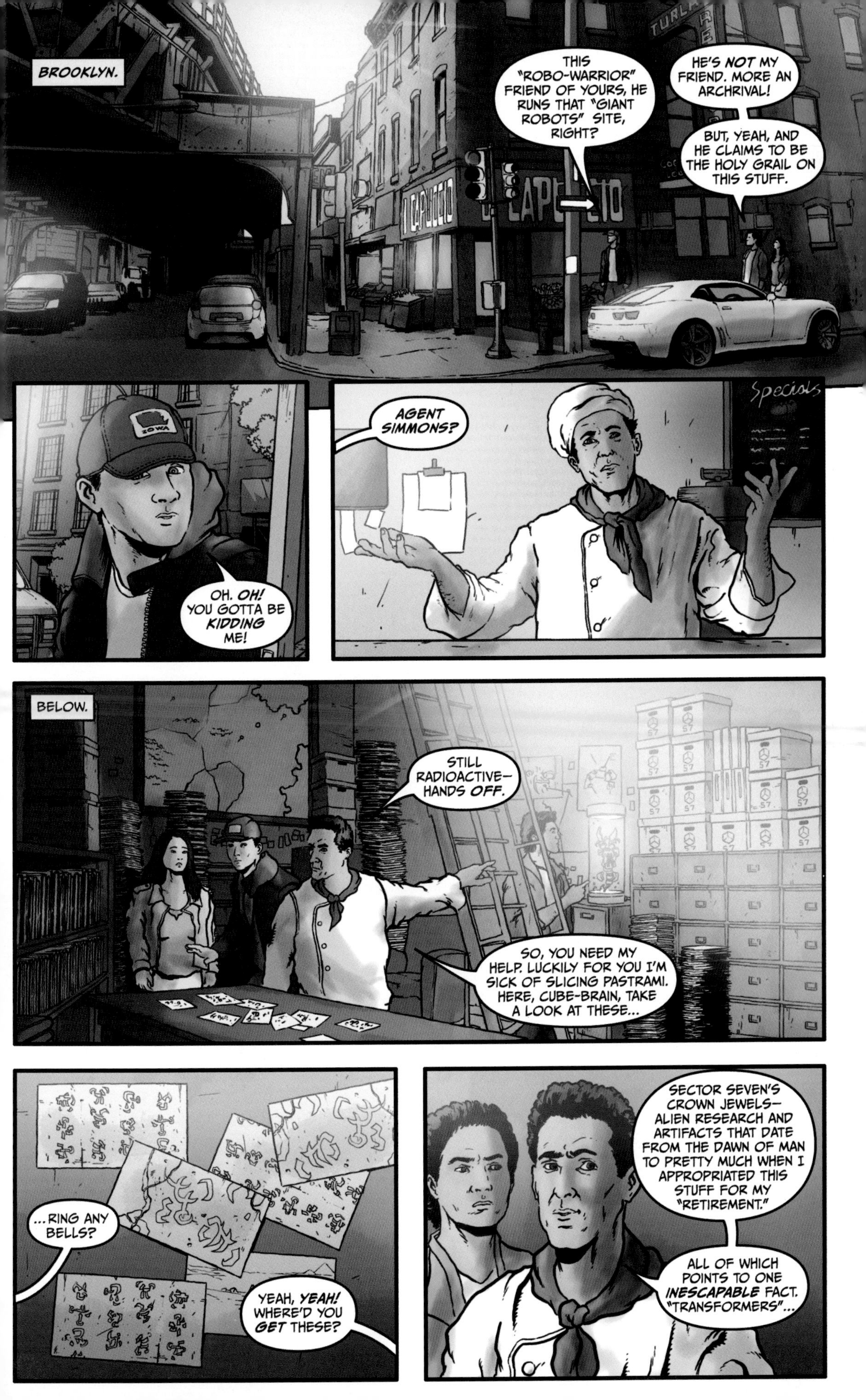
BROOKLYN.
THIS "ROBO-WARRIOR" FRIEND OF YOURS, HE RUNS THAT "GIANT ROBOTS" SITE, RIGHT?
HE'S NOT MY FRIEND. MORE AN ARCHRIVAL!
BUT, YEAH, AND HE CLAIMS TO BE THE HOLY GRAIL ON THIS STUFF.
OH. OH! YOU GOTTA BE KIDDING ME!
AGENT SIMMONS?
Specials
BELOW.
STILL RADIOACTIVE— HANDS OFF.
SO, YOU NEED MY HELP. LUCKILY FOR YOU I'M SICK OF SLICING PASTRAMI. HERE, CUBE-BRAIN, TAKE A LOOK AT THESE...
...RING ANY BELLS?
YEAH, YEAH! WHERE'D YOU GET THESE?
SECTOR SEVEN'S CROWN JEWELS— ALIEN RESEARCH AND ARTIFACTS THAT DATE FROM THE DAWN OF MAN TO PRETTY MUCH WHEN I APPROPRIATED THIS STUFF FOR MY "RETIREMENT."
ALL OF WHICH POINTS TO ONE INESCAPABLE FACT. "TRANSFORMERS"...

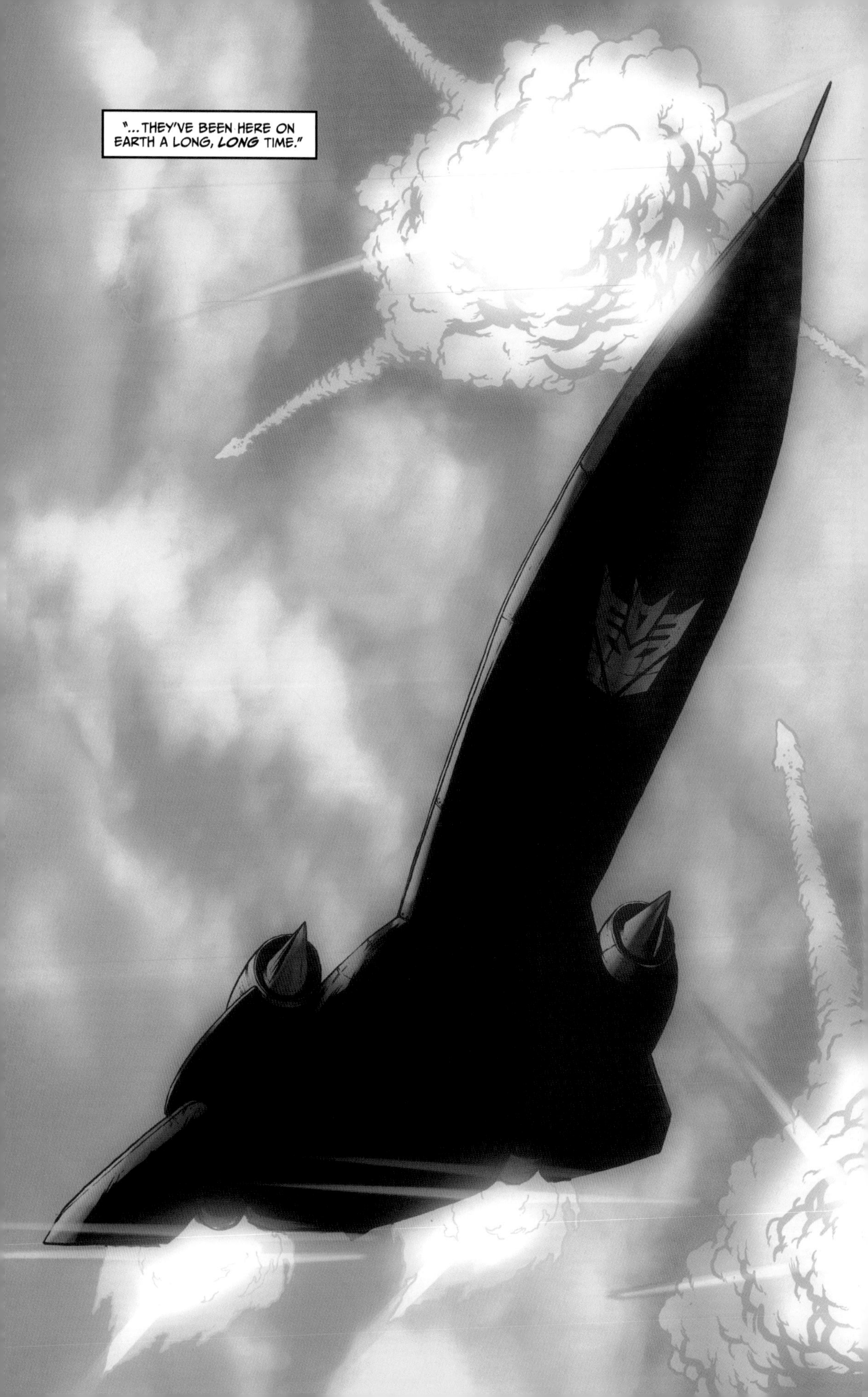
"...THEY'VE BEEN HERE ON EARTH A LONG, LONG TIME."